AF269842

Sound Moves

Kaitlyn Duling

rourkeeducationalmedia.com

SCHOOL to HOME
CONNECTIONS

BEFORE AND DURING READING ACTIVITIES

Before Reading: *Building Background Knowledge and Vocabulary*

Building background knowledge can help children process new information and build upon what they already know. Before reading a book, it is important to tap into what children already know about the topic. This will help them develop their vocabulary and increase their reading comprehension.

Questions and Activities to Build Background Knowledge:

1. Look at the front cover of the book and read the title. What do you think this book will be about?
2. What do you already know about this topic?
3. Take a book walk and skim the pages. Look at the table of contents, photographs, captions, and bold words. Did these text features give you any information or predictions about what you will read in this book?

Vocabulary: *Vocabulary Is Key to Reading Comprehension*

Use the following directions to prompt a conversation about each word.

- Read the vocabulary words.
- What comes to mind when you see each word?
- What do you think each word means?

Vocabulary Words:
- *eardrums*
- *gases*
- *vibrate*
- *volume*

During Reading: *Reading for Meaning and Understanding*

To achieve deep comprehension of a book, children are encouraged to use close reading strategies. During reading, it is important to have children stop and make connections. These connections result in deeper analysis and understanding of a book.

 ## Close Reading a Text

During reading, have children stop and talk about the following:

- Any confusing parts
- Any unknown words
- Text to text, text to self, text to world connections
- The main idea in each chapter or heading

Encourage children to use context clues to determine the meaning of any unknown words. These strategies will help children learn to analyze the text more thoroughly as they read.

When you are finished reading this book, turn to the last page for an **After Reading Activity**.

Table of Contents

Hearing Sound

Listen. Sound is all around!

I turn on the radio.

Music fills the air!

Sometimes sound is loud.

Sometimes it is quiet. This is called its **volume**.

Sound Waves

A guitar's strings
vibrate.

The vibrations cause sound waves.

You can't see sound waves. But you can make them!

We make sound waves with
our voices.

13

Sound waves go into your ears. They vibrate your **eardrums**. Your brain gets a signal. It helps you understand the sound.

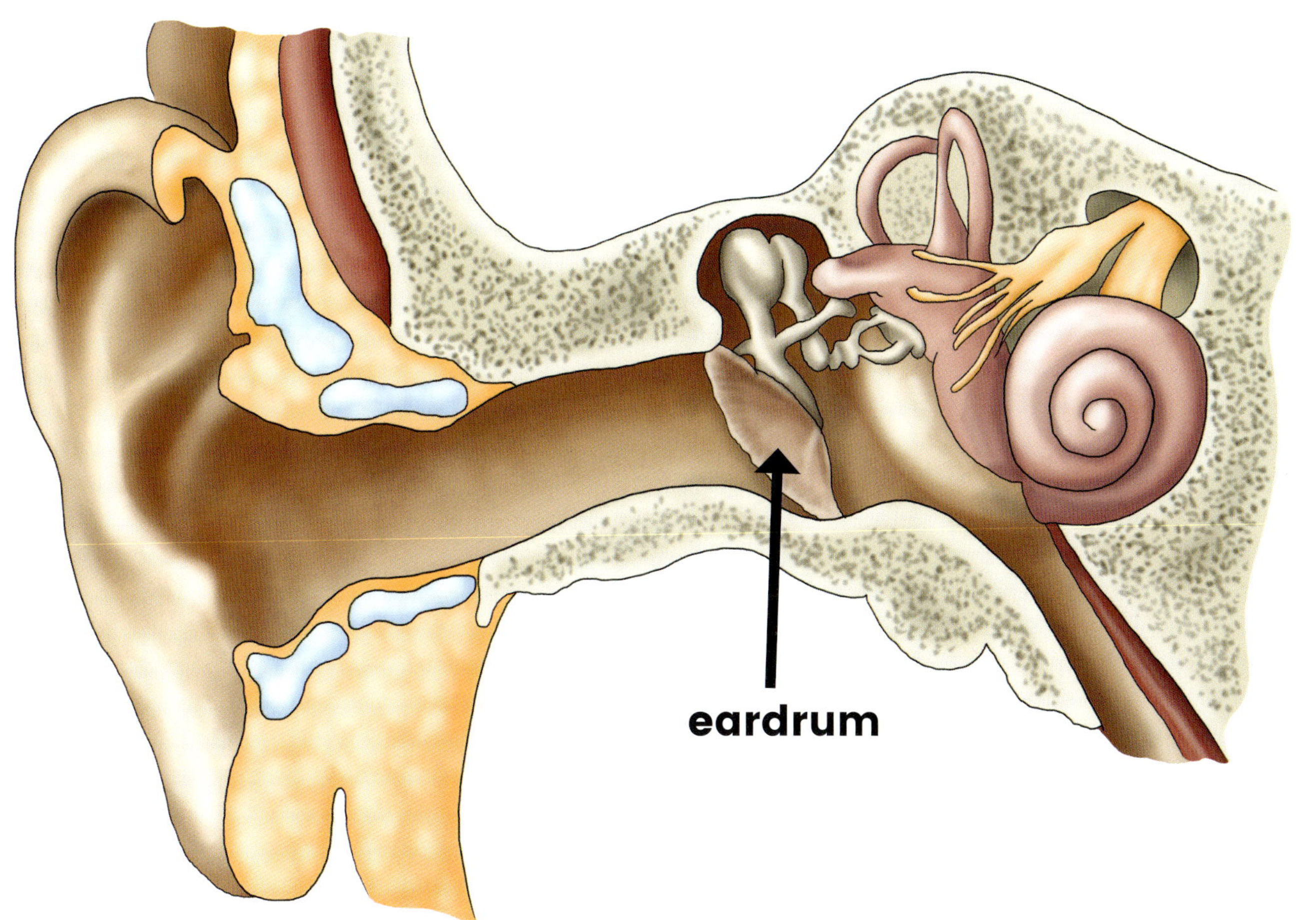

eardrum

Moving Through Matter

Sound waves can move through matter.

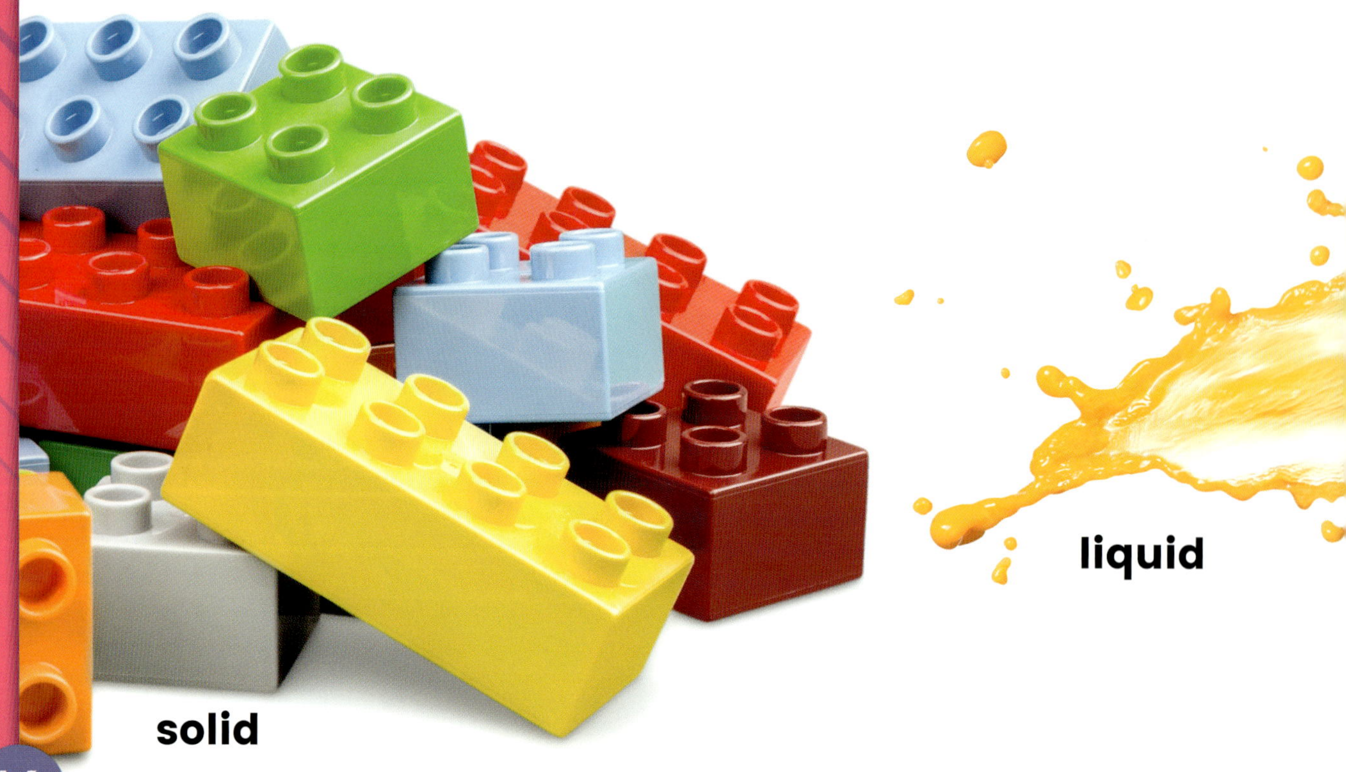

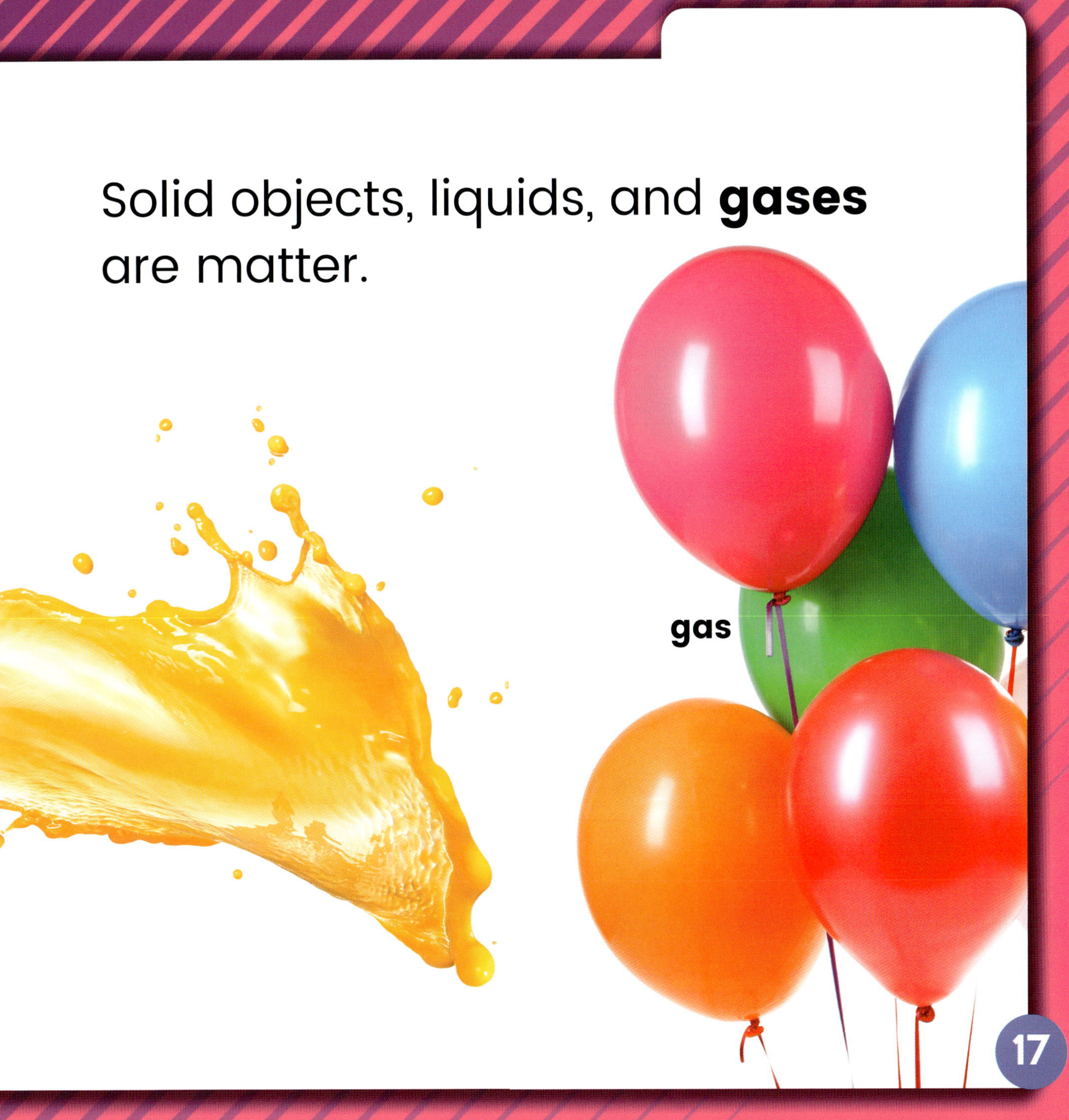

Solid objects, liquids, and **gases** are matter.

17

Sound waves move through the air.

They can move through a glass
of water.

19

If we play music loud enough, sound waves can move through walls.

That is beautiful music!

Photo Glossary

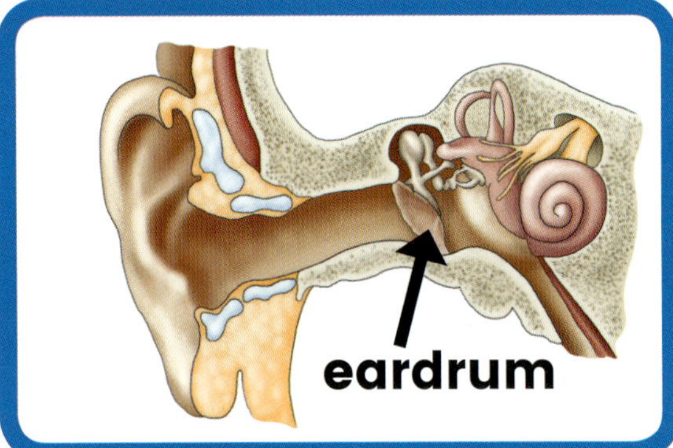

eardrums (EER-druhms): The membranes in each middle ear that vibrate in response to sound waves.

gases (GAS-iz): Substances, such as air, that will spread to fill any space that contains them.

vibrate (VYE-brate): To move back and forth quickly.

volume (VAHL-yoom): Loudness.

Water Music

Listen closely to learn how water can affect the size of sound waves as they pass through.

Supplies

six identical glasses or jars

water

spoon

Directions

1. Fill the first glass with just a little water.
2. Pour more water into the next glass, and the next. The last glass should be nearly full.
3. Gently tap on each glass with your spoon. What do you hear? How do the different amounts of water change the sounds?
4. Make up a simple song using the different musical sounds you've created. Bravo!

Index

About the Author

Kaitlyn Duling is an avid reader and writer who grew up in Illinois. She now resides in Washington, D.C., where she loves to dance to music! Kaitlyn has written over 60 books for children and teens. You can learn more about her at www.kaitlynduling.com.

After Reading Activity

Put some plastic wrap tightly over a large bowl. Sprinkle some uncooked rice on top. Then, use a metal spoon to hit a metal pan. The sound waves will make the plastic wrap vibrate. The rice will dance! This is one way to see sound waves in action.

Library of Congress PCN Data

Sound Moves / Kaitlyn Duling
(My Physical Science Library)
ISBN 978-1-73161-411-7 (hard cover)(alk. paper)
ISBN 978-1-73161-206-9 (soft cover)
ISBN 978-1-73161-516-9 (e-Book)
ISBN 978-1-73161-621-0 (e-Pub)
Library of Congress Control Number: 2019932067

Rourke Educational Media
Printed in the United States of America,
North Mankato, Minnesota

www.rourkeeducationalmedia.com

Edited by: Kim Thompson
Produced by Blue Door Education for Rourke Educational Media.
Cover and interior design by: Nicola Stratford

Photo Credits: Cover logo: frog © Eric Phol, test tube © Sergey Lazarev, cover tab art © siridhata, cover photos: girl © Africa Studio, background © bestfoto77, page background art © Zaie; page 5 © Africa Studio; Pages 6-7 and 20 music notes © Pavel K, page 5 © matka_Wariatka; page 8 © Littlekidmoment, page 9 © TY Lim; page 10 © Cora Mueller, page 11 © Joshua David Treisner; page 12 © Aaron Ama, page 13 © New Africa, page 12-13 sound waves © © HappyPictures; page 15 © miha de; page 16-17 legos © Billion Photos, orange juice © ifong, balloons © Africa Studio; page 18 © Elenamiv, page 19 © Kowit Lanchu; page 20 © fotoslaz, page 21 © Evgeniia Trushkova All images from Shutterstock.com